Written by
JERRY ZUCKERMAN

Illustrated by
JAMES SIEGFRIED

Dr. Z's Menagerie
Published by Jerry Zuckerman
For more information visit
www.drzmenagerie.com

ISBN: 978-0-69271-951-0

Text copyright © 2016 by Jerry Zuckerman

Illustrations copyright © 2016 by James Siegfried

Cover design and illustrations by Jim Siegfried
Interior layout and production by Gary A Rosenberg • www.thebookcouple.com

Printed in the United States of America

Introduction

Dr. Z is a wonderful, whimsical character. With degrees in veterinary science and psychology, he solves a multitude of problems in the animal kingdom.

In the third of the Dr. Z's Menagerie books, Dr. Z continues to solve the unusual problems of various animals. With clever rhymes and imaginative solutions, he once again comes to their rescue.

Dr. Z's solutions are certainly unique, as you will see in the stories within.

A zebra by the name of Loren
Didn't like her stripes.
Her behavior was somewhat foreign.
She was hardly a stereotype.

Ever since she was a tot
She wanted to have polka dots.

Not liking stripes made Loren unique.
The other zebras called her a freak.

The older zebras in the pack
Thought all she needed was a good sound whack.

But the younger zebras thought she was sick.
Perhaps medication would do the trick.

The only course of action on which they could agree
Was to take her for treatment to Dr. Z.

They were all fed up, they'd had their fill.
They hoped he'd prescribe some kind of pill.

When Loren explained her situation
Dr. Z rejected medication.

Instead he gave her a special shot
Which turned her stripes right into dots.

Her return to the pack came as quite a surprise.
The zebras could hardly believe their eyes.
The elder zebras who used to gripe
Now looked at Loren without her stripes.

Do you think they were mad? They were not.
They were proud of Loren and her polka dots.
For Loren's a zebra like all the rest.
She's just a zebra differently dressed.

Sonny the Hyena

There was a hyena named Sonny
Who didn't like to laugh.
To Sonny nothing was funny.
Not even a long-necked giraffe.

According to reliable rumor
When Sonny was a child
He had no sense of humor.
And he very rarely smiled.

His parents became so concerned
They brought him to a physician.
In hopes that he would discern
A cure for Sonny's condition.

They brought him to Dr. Z's clinic
To hear what he had to say.
Was Sonny an incurable cynic?
Could Dr. Z help him find his way?

The reason he had no sense of humor
On the X-ray it was clearly shown.
Dr. Z didn't find a tumor.
Sonny was missing his funny bone.

It should come as no surprise
Dr. Z had funny bone supplies.

After just a couple of tries
He even found the perfect size.

It wasn't too big
Just the size of a knuckle.
But as soon as it went in him
Sonny let out a chuckle.

To best describe his new condition
He has a sunny disposition!

Owl Ben

Once there was an owl
Sitting in a tree.
He wore a constant scowl.
He was as unhappy as could be.

He went by the name of Ben.
And on a scale of 1 to 10
With 10 standing for the most fun
Ben was a number 1.

The other owls tried and tried
To help their fellow fowl.
Eventually their efforts died.
And they threw in the towel.

One suggested therapy
As a last resort.
So they sent him off to Dr. Z
And awaited his report.

Dr. Z wore many hats.
He had more than one degree.
He was a veterinarian and on top of that
An expert in psychology.

His work in animal behavior
Was known both wide and far.
He was the animal kingdom's savior.
And a veterinary rising star.

Dr. Z said, "Lets begin."
"First we must balance your yang and your yin."
He had Ben do a yoga pose
As well as breathe through just his nose.
Then he mumbled some mystic chants
To put Ben in a zen-like trance.

He had Ben lay down on the couch.
And asked a question or two.
To learn why Ben was such a grouch.
And how Dr. Z could get through.

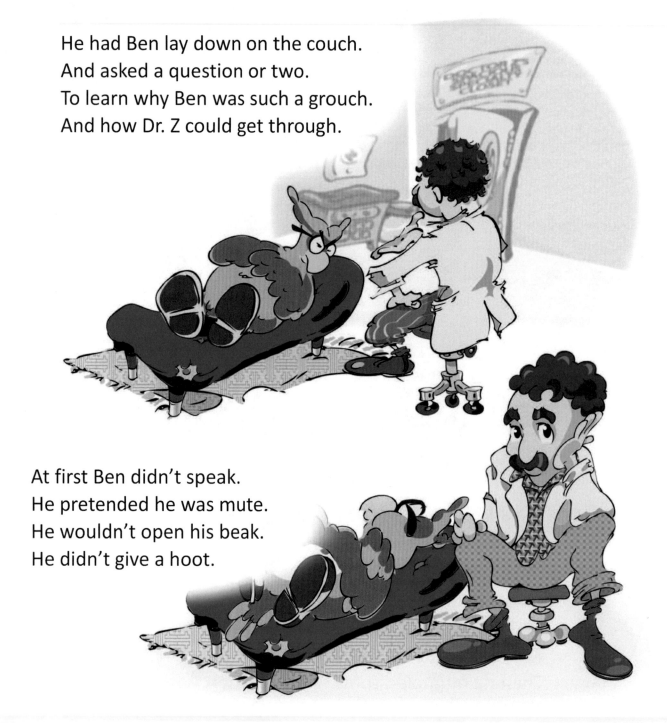

At first Ben didn't speak.
He pretended he was mute.
He wouldn't open his beak.
He didn't give a hoot.

Dr. Z gave Ben a drink
Made of water and a mystery juice.
It made his eyes go blink blink blink.
It made his beak come loose.

31

Now Ben felt he had no choice.
Today would be the day.
And so he opened up his voice
And this is what he had to say.

"The first time I tried flying
I ran into a tree."
"I landed hard and started crying.
Which every owl could see."

"And ever since that day
I've had this attitude."
"I guess you'd probably say
I've been in a foul, fowl mood."

When Dr. Z heard his tale
A tear came to his eye.
But he knew he would prevail.
And now I'll tell you why.

Dr. Z had probed his past.
Looking for a clue.
He found the answer at long last.
And knew just what to do.

The Doctor didn't hesitate.
He took Ben to Tibet.
There Ben learned to meditate
From a guru that they met.

Ben returned a brand new owl.
He no longer wears a scowl.
He flies the forest in a toga
And teaches all the owlets yoga.

His attitude is really great.
And he made himself a vow.
Every day to meditate
And start living in the now!

The End

About the Author

Jerry Zuckerman is the creator and author of Dr. Z. In his youth, Jerry was a racquetball pro and now works as a financial advisor. *Dr. Z's Menagerie #3* is the third book in the Dr. Z series. Jerry lives in St. Louis with his wife, Linda, and dog, Spike.

About the Illustrator

James Siegfried is the illustrator of the Dr. Z series. His imagination and sense of humor is showcased on every page he illustrates. Jim also lives in St. Louis with his family and has been drawing, illustrating, and painting for most of his life.

Made in the USA
Lexington, KY
05 March 2019